The Rhyme Mine

A Life in Verse

By Richard A. Davis

Published in 2023.

Other books by this author:

God, I Don't Get It: Critical Thinking on Critical Questions

Internal Affairs: How to Mend a Wounded Soul

Cover: Soglio, Switzerland

ISBN 979-8-218-96227-2

Dedicated to my Susan Lynn-spiration.

CONTENTS

INTRODUCTION

It takes time to write a book. A lot of time. This one has been in the works for 56 years. Since before computers and smart phones. Back when pencils, pens, and scraps of paper were an aspiring writer's tools. When I was 17, I had the aspiration; all I needed was the inspiration. And then I found it. I found her.

Halfway through my senior year of high school, I met an attractive girl a year younger. She not only caught my eye, she caught all of me. Mind. Body. And soul. Her blonde hair, olive skin, graceful manner, and blue eyes brought out the poet in me. Young love (aka hormones) is a powerful thing. I was suddenly empowered by my love for Susan Lynn Nordquist. I had known puppy love, but this was different. I quickly realized that Susan Lynn would be my one, true love.

Susan captured my heart. Now what could I do to capture hers? I wasn't a star athlete. I wasn't tall, dark, and handsome. Tall maybe, but not the other two. I was a new kid in a big suburban school, having moved from a small town in Iowa to the metropolis of Minneapolis. But that didn't score any points for me. I had to find something to win the attention and affection of this fetching lass. Then it hit me. I had a skill. I knew how to use words.

My mother was an English major in college, and she raised her seven kids to read books, play word games, appreciate culture, love music, go to church, bring home good grades, and develop memory skills. Mom exposed us to nursery rhymes, fables, fairy tales and tall tales. She introduced us to Frost, Longfellow, Tennyson, Clement Clark Moore ("The Night Before Christmas"), and many others. My favorite by far was Dr. Seuss. I think we had all his books, and I memorized his poems. I can still recite a few. My mother equipped me with an arsenal of literary arrows to rival Cupid's. And my target was Susan's heart.

I began to write poems for my new girlfriend. Many poems. Love poems. Dark poems. Light poems. Short poems. Long poems. Flattering poems. Apologetic poems. Sensuous poems. Silly poems. Religious poems. Sacrilegious poems. I found that expressing my adolescent moods in rhyme and rhythm was both fulfilling and fruitful. Poetry provided an emotional outlet, and therein was the fulfillment. Better yet, poetry ripened the fruits of romance. I wrote the poems and Susan kept them, recording them in two handwritten volumes.

I still have those volumes. I also still have the lady who collected them. That's the punchline. A memorable poem should have a punchline and mine did. I won the lady's heart...along with her hand in marriage. Never underestimate the power of poetry.

In the pages that follow are the resurrected poems that have been buried in boxes and on bookshelves for over half a century. I've sorted through them, tossing out some and polishing up others. What emerged was an introspective retrospective of my life, my love, and my faith.

The teenaged poet is now an old poet. But I'm glad to say that my heart is still beating and the rhymes are still flowing, inspired by my lovely lady, by my God, and by my timeless passion for life. Take the time. Read my rhyme. I hope you'll find some gems in mine.

-- Richard A. Davis, Poet

THE NIGHT AND THE RIVER

We meet here at the river, beneath the sunset glow.

We touch and taste each other, beside its soothing flow.

As darkness falls and breezes rise to welcome in the night,

We shed the stress, forget the rest, and bathe in evening light.

The darkness loves the river; I'm certain this is true.

I've seen them close together, as I've been close to you.

I've heard their quiet whispers and watched their glances touch,

And laughed their laugh, and cried their cry, and found in you as much.

The night sees us together, in shadows we embrace,

It takes our breath then sends the wind to kiss the water's face.

The heavens know I love you; the river knows it's true.

They hear us talk. They see us walk. They feel me close to you.

We sense the river's hidden strength within its constant flow,

A current we can never push, like life, we watch it go.

The darkness and the river. They sing in harmony.

Their voices blend at every bend and pour your charms on me.

THE GOOD OLD LION

I don't hear the lion anymore,

or the heavens shaken by his roar.

No panting breath or growling low;

Where is that threat I used to know?

May the good old lion lift my spirit high.

May the volume of his voice be echoed 'cross the sky.

May the good old lion blast his fearful cry.

Rousing those resigned to live by merely getting by.

I need to know who's in control,

when silence mutes my soul.

I long to hear the lion's songs,

Inspired to right my wrongs.

Until the day when all this madness ends,

I'll stand beside the mighty lion's friends.

We're in his pride and by his side,

He guards our doors and prowls our floors;

Under his protection we'll abide.

I'll love and serve the lion,

to keep him fierce and free.

And when I rise, he'll hear my cries,

and arm the beast in me.

A CYNIC'S PSALM

I cruise round town in my limousine,

The gawkers turn their heads.

They like the way I swoop in my jet-black coupe,

And then the rumors spread.

Oh, how the rumors spread.

I've got a posh townhouse on the beach,

A stable full of women with jewels on each.

But wrapped in gems galore,

They always ask for more.

With envy they beseech, for gifts beyond their reach.

Living large with a troubled soul.

Who's in control? Who's in control?

Living large with a troubled soul.

Piling treasures on my own.

I'm off to Rome to buy a home.

My tailored clothes are deemed the best,

And chains of gold adorn my chest.

My lofty friends count dividends,

While lawyers tie up all loose ends.

I know I should be happy; the world is on my string,

But silencing my conscience is more than challenging.

Living large with a troubled soul.

Who's in control? Who's in control?

Living large with a troubled soul.

I've got money in the bank.

I've got social rank.

All my art is rare; watch the masses stare,

But late at night come the pangs of fright.

When the whisper asks, "Who cares?"

They love my wealth, but they sap my health,

These are parasites, I see.

Their hands are out, and I have no doubt,

They don't give a damn about me.

No, they don't give a damn about me.

So, who is left to give a damn?

Such as I am, who gives a damn?

Such as I am, such as I am, who gives a damn about me?

THE TIDE OF PRIDE

The love I have for you may not be simple or divine,

For what I feel depends upon this crazy world of mine.

Cause if I wish, I'll confuse it.

And if I want, I'll abuse it.

Right or wrong, I will choose it.

But, oh Dear Lord, don't let me lose it.

Fickle feelings, fickle love,

Rolling on the tide of pride.

Ebb and flow, away I go,

Dear Lord, please ease my ride.

The praise I give to you is shallow, not sincere.

My words are empty-hearted prose, devotion nowhere near.

When all intentions fail me,

I then expose the frail me.

My sharp-tongued habits nail me.

Dear Lord, why can't I hail Thee?

Fickle feelings, fickle love,

Rolling on the tide of pride.

Ebb and flow, away I go,

Dear Lord, please calm my ride.

Running long, but never strong.

Always right, but never wrong.

Lies in life, but truth in song.

I'm creeping, Lord, not keeping, Lord,

Take the rudder, fill the sail,

For left alone, I always fail.

Fickle feelings, fickle love,

Rolling on the tide of pride.

Ebb and flow, away I go,

Dear Lord, please guide my ride.

HOBO EYES

It's a perked up city,

Polished fine and pretty.

There's coffee in my cup, and I'm all hyped up.

I'm sitting in my stall,

Behind a plate glass wall,

While the street beggars mingle in the heat.

 There is no disguise for those hobo eyes,

No escaping their burning glare.

It's the pain and the blame of the jungle game;

It's the world where nothing's fair.

 As I'm sipping on my brew,

I can't see you,

Cuz the coffee in my cup has me all hyped up.

 You slowly saunter by,

On a different high,

Then you grab what you will, and we all sit still.

 It's a jacked-up city,

Full of sin and pity.

There's coffee in our cups and we're all hyped up.

 Here inside our border,

There is no law and order,

The only rule is to take more than give…just to live.

There is no disguise for those hobo eyes,

No escaping their burning glare.

It's the pain and the blame of the jungle game;

It's the world where nothing's fair.

THE POTION

She gave me all her sweetness,

A measured mix of love,

And spiced it up with yesterdays

We think together of.

She put a pinch of silly in

And added thoughtfulness,

With just a dab of mystery

To make me always guess.

A spoon of powdered whispers,

A cup of silent glance,

A drop of understanding—

A hug, a kiss, perchance.

While stirring up the potion

To make the contents blend,

She added but one teardrop

To help things never end.

When things aren't going smoothly, when things aren't working out, I take this dose of medicine to clear all pain—all doubt.

DREAM THOUGHTS

The starlings searched the lawn today,

The squirrels cleaned their house.

The scarecrow chased the crows away,

The black cat killed a mouse.

Autumn tells the leaves to fall,

While spring must prompt them grow.

Summer makes its sunshine call,

As winter summons snow.

The church's cross is weathered from days turned off and on.

And rows of headstones planted mark boxes in the lawn.

A tree branch breaks the moonlight,

To trace lines on your face,

As in my eyes the glow-bright of your reflections trace.

From here will start our travels,

To places dreamed, not seen.

As what has been unravels,

Tomorrow's edge is keen.

THE CHALET

A valley lies in Switzerland,

The one we're dreaming of,

Where meadows, streams, and breezes play,

With snow-capped peaks above.

A little village nestles at the entrance of a pass,

Surrounded by the shepherds' flocks,

That graze the meadow grass.

A chalet waits there for us,

In blue light from the moon.

Its vigil is a brief one;

We both will be there soon.

GROWTH

Times will come and burden me with tasks that I must do.

And years will fade like day and night before my life is through.

The hand, Responsibility, will grasp me by the arm,

Then drop me into what it will, in happiness or harm.

For as a feather nearing flame, the life of man compares.

Our precious moments wilt away, while on our souls, time wears.

And if you pluck a plant from ground, it dies from lack of soil.

But I, in You, have taken root no power on earth can spoil.

<u>TWO FRUITS</u>

Beyond the narrow river,

As far as you can see,

There is a separate forest,

Where God did plant a tree.

The seed was introduction,

The fertile soil was youth;

The rainfall, understanding;

The living sunshine, truth.

A single flower blossomed,

Atop the full-grown tree,

It stretched to touch the sun rays,

Then flourished strong and free.

Two fruits grew from the blossom,

On one stem, side by side.

They still are ripe though every other leaf and limb have died.

DAWN TO DUSK

I don't know where I'm going,

I don't know where to turn.

I only know I love you,

Life teaches me. I learn.

A storm can bend the willow,

And make it bow still more.

But time can make the branches straight,

Much stronger than before.

I once threw sand on fires,

To make the flames die out.

I used to walk by rivers,

And wander all about.

A sunrise lights the future.

A sunset seals the past.

Together only they can say

How long our love will last.

AN EMPTY, THOUGHTFUL STARE

When one is gone and one's alone, together they will be.

Not distance, time, nor parting can melt a memory.

The moon can see that all's the same, the earth, the sky, the trees.

Then by the river's quiet flow, a single form he sees.

A figure leans against an elm, his gaze a thoughtful stare.

The flutter hum of wind through leaves runs fingers through his hair.

A bird will cry a warning, the cave will cool the sand;

Yet nothing in the woods can warm the lonely lover's hand.

When one returns, the other's there; together they will be.

Not distance, time, nor parting can melt a memory.

SOMEWHERE

A little boy once asked of heaven,

"Oh, is there such a place? And is there really joy and peace,

Divinity and grace?

And are there hearts that love a man for what he is inside?

And are there places flowers grow where grieving parents cried?"

I lowered my arm and took his hand,

To lead him to a brook.

And sitting near the gentle flow,

I read to him The Book.

But to the child its words were thick,

Its thoughts too deep to see.

So carefully I laid it down,

And took him on my knee.

I showed him where the robins perch,

And where the angels sing.

I told him why the crickets chirp,

And when the church bells ring.

I showed him where the rabbits run,

And where the sunlight shines,

And where the moon will rise at night,

To light the paths he climbs.

He stretched his arms around my neck,

And whispered in my ear,

"I think I know where heaven is;

It's neither far nor near.

It's somewhere, hidden, in between,

And just beyond our reach,

And God has planted clues for us,

Like seashells on the beach.

And when we have our pockets full,

We run, returning home,

To show our Father what we've found,

And how much we have grown."

He then breathed deeply, closed his eyes,

And smiled as if he knew,

That something more than questioning

Had set his course anew.

The walls collapsed, amid his gasps,

The wondering child was free

To gaze with trust--as we all must--into eternity.

<u>BLOSSOMS</u>

One bud blossoms happiness,

And wants the world to know.

The other waits by patiently,

To have her petals show.

For one has found life's value,

And beauty she has seen,

The other, quite aware of both,

Attempts to be, not seem.

Approach each bloom with caution,

And take a peek inside.

The one has nectar flowing,

The other stamen's dried.

The sweetest flower attracts the bee to help it reach maturity.

The bloom which will not nectar give must fight alone to grow and live.

Only God can raise them both, according to their natural oath.

As spring is birth, and winter death,

In love alone is life.

WHEN SOMEONE CRIES

Have you ever gazed into a teardrop?

I have.

A teardrop is a crystal ball.

And the best place to view a tear is on a warm cheek.

I now see many things within.

Sometimes I see love.

Sometimes I see pain.

The surface shows the sun;

Within I find the rain.

What becomes of a teardrop?

It flows down the face,

And trickles to the chin;

And there it's fanned by soft, warm breath,

Then quivers, shrinks, and dies.

I often catch each tear too late,

And only when she cries.

OF BIRTH AND AGE

I saw a child walk in the wind,

With young man's face and old man's pace.

I saw his hair dance in the breeze,

Bushed full and red on thinning head.

I saw him skip and kick a stone,

Then lean with pain on hickory cane.

I heard him laugh and shout and cheer,

And saw him smile, then rest a while.

I watched him tug a fair girl's hair,

Then lift her spirits in the air.

And then, I saw him kiss the bride,

Aglow with passion's flames inside.

Without a sound, he hit the ground.

Now flowers lace his lifeless face.

A child conceived.

He sleeps. He cries.

A man is born.

He lives. He dies.

SEEDS OF FATE

In sorrow, there is happiness.

In love, there is despair.

In heartache, there is laughter.

In illness, there is care.

Our fickle thoughts can change our lives,

Impulses change our world.

Offense can bring a banner down,

Replaced by fears unfurled.

A cloud can blot the glaring sun,

Absorbing all its glow.

The moon can shed its eerie light,

Upon December snow.

God's hand stirs the ocean depths,

And makes the currents cease,

He fans the flames of troubled souls,

Then sooths them into peace.

The Sower plants the seeds of fate,

That grow in hungry minds.

The Grower waters thirsty crops,

All colors, shapes, and kinds.

And if our roots are severed

And our fruit begins to spoil,

The Lord bends down, transplanting us in firmer, richer soil.

FOR WHAT OUR GOD MAY SEND

A silent moon.

A fragment cloud.

The starlight beamed in bits,

To rooming houses far below,

With false front parapets.

To searching eyes,

To quiet moans,

To children lost in sleep,

Illuminating drying fields

Where weary farmers reap.

A town.

A street.

A corner light.

A gentle evening roar.

Our friend is pounding frantically

Upon his neighbor's door.

"Don't let him in; he's full of sin.

Let's leave him in the dark."

For all we know, he's wicked.

We hear his piercing bark.

I gently reach to touch her hand,

And tell her of my love.

But winter winds with ice and snow

Attack us from above.

The cemetery on the hill

Was made my brother's bed.

And now he runs, alive at last,

With scores of others dead.

Your father tipped his head that day.

I saw him in the pew.

I stretched out on the hillside grass,

And sang a song with you.

With joy, we danced the tune he wrote

Before he paid our bill.

We vowed to keep the legacy,

Recorded in his will.

We took our bag of bread and cheese,

And dined beside a lake,

Which mirrored dark reflections

Of the lives it dared to take.

I've heard a voice profoundly state

The thoughts our minds perceive,

And seen the fools who blindly mate

When lustful hearts conceive.

Yet far away a rainbow frowns.

For far away, there's war.

The cratered streets are watered down.

The warriors' eyes are sore.

A quiet night. A lonely hill.

A boy and girl in sight.

Their eyes distracted by the moon,

With captivating light.

A time. A place.

An everyday, with daybreak round the bend.

A kiss. A cry.

As now we pray for what our God may send.

CRYSTAL WAR

Beneath the twilight snowflake war,

The battlefield lies.

Fluorescent clouds upon its crest,

Neath languid, lurking skies.

With crystal armies spinning in,

They randomly collide,

While hiding, oh so carefully, their chilling fears inside.

They twist their heads and stretch their arms,

Engaging with the foe,

Then fall, embraced by comrades dead,

In fluffy mounds of snow.

THE PARTLY ROOM

The naïve observations of the boy behind the broom,

Preparing reservations in the stained and dusty room.

This day of festive cooking has been purchased by the King,

But vagrants still are looking for a higher price to bring.

Fine powder mounts up inches deep,

On branches of the tree,

As colored lights blink on and off,

Impersonating glee.

Bustling halls and glistening walls

bring carolers to the door.

And in the glass the sand-grain falls,

While old folks beg for more.

A sleepless infant vainly cries,

To nudge the souls awake;

Lest in their dreams the baby dies,

And strained relations break.

Devoid of cares, the young boy stares,

But then resumes his sweeping.

He's never free of such debris,

When secrets he is keeping.

The rituals roll to gain control,

Of every anxious heart.

But one thing's clear again this year:

The end is just the start.

The urge to act obscures the fact,

That nothing's ever clean.

Sweep as we will, it's useless still,

Until the Lamb is seen.

FINGERS

You told me that you loved me once.

And once when you were cold,

You chanted vows of future bliss,

And made your mother old.

You wove a nest of tiny flowers,

The bird of ivory seeks,

While tender tips of blushing warmth

Drew laugh-lines on my cheeks.

We know a mountain by its slope,

And memorize its face.

Its marks of wisdom deeply set,

For seasons to erase.

But streams of growth will still remain,

Though storms and drought may pass,

Like finger pictures that we drew

On panes of foggy glass.

NOW, TELL ME

'Twas love, I heard the prophet say,

That made the wisdom grow,

And softened touch,

And glazed the eyes,

And hushed the whispers low.

For love, it is a meadow,

Where boundless senses dance,

And fears disperse,

And worries hide,

As new life finds its chance.

A chance to thrive where people seldom see that this is how God meant the world to be.

Now, tell me why you love me,

And then why I love you,

And time will tell the secrets of eternity for two.

For no man knows, as once one did,

But no man really knows.

SPRING

In spring the baby blossoms hide,

Concealing all their doubts inside,

Then, gaining courage, gaining strength,

Emerge to be a flower.

<u>YOUR FACE</u>

In your face I find a mirror,

A flawless silver pane,

With images so sharp and clear

They shine through April rain.

And in your voice I hear a song,

With notes I've heard before,

Arranged in tones so smooth and long

That even larks adore.

With every touch I feel the breeze

That night brings from the sea,

Awakening my dormant soul to praise a memory.

For in your eyes I've found a prayer,

The heart light that you give,

As with you comes the morning air,

A stronger will to live.

THE SEARCH

Our search for hope was endless, we looked for crumbs and clues.

Our spirit found no resting place, except to mend our shoes.

We lost our balance, every step, uncertain what to seek,

Until we met the lonely man, who bade us not to speak.

Before our eyes, day turned to night;

The man was stripped of all his might.

The bounty flowing from his heart,

Paid off the past and bought our start.

The blood on wood where flesh was nailed,

Exposed the spot where hubris failed.

The empire built by boastful fools, collapsed beneath its godless rules.

Our fruitless search has ended; we've found whom we can trust, we've left the haze inside the maze to walk beside the just.

We've shed the leash of mammon and fled the bonds of fate;

We've now escaped the famine and no longer take the bait.

As others search from perch to perch, and fly from nest to nest,

We're here to stay, from day to day, the Comforter our guest.

INSPIRATION

You said my eyes turned green when I cried.

Usually, they are a dull gray.

And sometimes I smile at you, while other times you <u>tell</u> me that I smiled at you.

It's strange—strange because your eyes are always bright and blue, and I always see your smiles.

I never wrote poetry before, you know.

I never wrote music before you.

Your life is my life and mine is yours, and, from this, springs our mutual future.

I also was ignorant before I knew you, merely full of arrogant knowledge.

In Sunday school, people told me of God; in solitude, you taught me about Him.

Who composes art? The artist or his model?

The beauty is in the work, and the work is by the artist.

Yet, the work <u>is</u> the model.

Perspective channels art, and perception leads perspective.

One short rhyme this time, but always looking.

MAGIC

When swirling forces lift our heads,

And storms rise from our past,

Our souls are drawn to darker rooms,

Where memories were cast.

The sleepy voices sing a hymn,

It's one we've heard before;

While stoic faces turn away

To gaze upon the door.

I long to lay with you all day,

How dare I have such dreams;

For this is not the time or place

Beneath these sacred beams.

There's marbled sunshine everywhere,

There's dust and droning in the air…

But here we touch.

That magic touch.

That private thrill of ours.

The secret pact we cannot act,

Or so say lesser powers.

We've flourished in the open space,

At times we both recall,

Where once our bodies wrapped around

And felt no pain at all.

The verses that we read of love

May serve us as a crutch,

But we have found the healing balm:

The timeless, magic touch.

IF ONLY

Blinded by haze, we swim through our days,

Till tides cease and dry in the sun.

Ah, just to live on a whim,

Like careless men who leave kith and kin to attach to a lost someone else.

Oh, just to fly on a thought,

And drift without fear to a place that seems near but leads only somewhere else.

Ah, to touch a beating heart,

To be able to feel what is fragile and real with stained and calloused hands.

Oh, to grab the vagrant wind, to kite on the breeze that soars over the seas and then settle in distant lands.

Ah, to confirm Daniel's stand.

When the pride in the den backed down there and then, and vacancy fell on the throne.

Oh, that we might have known that the fullness of life is found in the strife, not in pleasures indulged in alone.

Beneficent breeds plant frail, dormant seeds which produce the most beautiful flowers.

THE TURNING

A common birth as Leo roared,

A brother's death as angels soared,

A springtime fog and winter's frost,

Turn young boys into men.

A helping hand when trouble's near,

A kiss to suffocate the fear,

And reams of light and shadowed dawns,

Turn young boys into men.

The whispers in an open ear,

Reflect a moment passing near,

Lost in darkness, stumbling steps,

Turn young boys into men.

A single child in classrooms bored,

Repenting to his waiting Lord,

His parents gone, his sleepless nights,

Turn young boys into men.

We've spent so little time together, yet it seems the hours are ours.

HIS LIFE

His life seeps away.

His soul gathers strength.

Prepared since his birth for this day.

His mother found joy in knowing her boy

Would have glories galore as his fate.

Just under her breath, she whispers a prayer.

She sings and she whispers a prayer.

She pleads for the best for the child at her breast,

To whom nature has given a tithe.

His calling from birth was here on the earth,

So that others could learn how to fly.

But now it is late. The end of the wait.

No pensive child dies without fears;

They mount through the fast-passing years.

Low dirges are sung, but not for the young,

It's the old folks who sing for their peers.

Each beat and each breath,

In defiance of death,

Provide us with constant protection.

Encircling our soul and sapping control,

They cease for our sweet resurrection.

The flight to the gate is never too late,

And the gatekeeper knows every name.

"You're cleansed of all sin, so please enter in.

I've risen. Now, child, do the same."

PLANS

You say you've made plans for the future,

Then so much the better for you.

For lives that flourish grow,

As eyes of dreamers glow.

And so much the better for you, little girl.

As lovers' whispers echo off barren valley walls,

The poet is inspired by his little china dolls.

TAKE ME BACK

Take me back to the hill,

Back to the field where maidens dance in velvet gowns,

And children laugh at paper clowns.

Take me back to the slope,

Back to the glen where young men sing a soothing tune,

And lovers kiss beneath the moon.

Take me back to the land,

Back to the paths where old folks take their evening walks,

And nods and smiles adorn their talks.

Take me back to the sea,

Back to horizons where beaches stretch for miles and miles,

And waves leap over tide-stained stiles.

Take me home.

Home to you.

Where comfort waits in pillows.

CELESTIAL

Resplendent flowers cease to grow when heaven's rains reside,

And ardent lovers cease to know their longing needs inside.

When good intentions prompt an arm to reach and pinch a bud,

That vain desire carries harm and drains the heart of blood.

Yet faith prevails in someone near,

That someone who disables fear.

The one who guards the spot that's weak,

And knows to listen more than speak.

Throughout the years of days we've spent

I've come to see she's heaven-sent.

For even in my darkest hour, she writes a note and sends a flower.

She hums a song and warms my hand; she prompts me pause to understand.

Inspired by her childlike truth, she fills me with the joy of youth.

I lay awake at night…sleeping with her. Will she be here forever?

<u>BESIDE THE LAKE</u>

Pensive staring from a dock,

Where weary waters lick at aging posts.

And I, gazing there through murky eyes,

At shuffling sandy bottoms,

With surging shapes of minnow-fish,

Who dart my grasp,

And disappear,

With sole intent to reappear

To tease my trapping hand.

I raise my gaze and fly to the moon.

Beholding cloudless nights in June with wonders spread above.

The pages turned from gusts of wind that mussed our drying hair.

As eternal sunlight stole the moisture there,

Changing into dew…ready by dawn to be rolled upon.

Blushing treetops warned of summer's fall.

Then with the snowflakes comes the call,

"Next spring awaits its time."

SKY WATCH

Just look at a star,

You'll see it glows.

Then squint, and as everyone knows, it grows.

A dull apathetic gloss,

A glass of glimmering light,

A lens of haze to hold our gaze until the close of night.

Not even clouds distort my view

On every timeless night with you;

The moon bursts through,

And straight and true,

The water runs, the ripples new.

I stretch to feel your velvet touch,

No wealth could offer me as much,

Of pure, profound contentment such.

The breezes rustle laden limbs,

As peep-holes form from time to time,

To make donations to our glance,

While fairies dance,

When given chance,

To join the crickets' song.

All night long.

I heard the echo of my voice,

Right then, as I whispered.

I spoke for only you to hear,

Not others near.

And yet, it does appear

That we have been alone.

Where is our star?

Behind the moon.

But it will shine again quite soon.

Just wait.

It's not too late…

We're here to ride the tides of fate.

NEGLECT

We're so engrossed in vanity that often we neglect to see,

How others, bearing equal gifts succumb to massive weight.

The fathers feed their starving children dry unleavened bread
while mothers stroke the bloated forms of infants lying dead.

Yet earth provides no rest to those with supplications said.

"Don't cry," we say, "on some fine day, the blight will go
away."

We fail to use our smokey mirror or ask the prophets what
they hear.

Instead, we punctuate our lives with sins beyond compare.

Audaciously, we ask for more while shaking fingers at the poor, convinced our stance is fair.

Before The Bench, we've dug a trench, to bury hidden shame.

How can we dare stand limp and stare at those without a name?

For soon a voice will fill the cleft,

And warn how little time is left.

Will we reply with practiced ease, "I noticed not the least of these?"

Then stripped of pride and vanity, we'll lift our heads...and see.

ONCE

Once I held my mother's hand while Father walked ahead,

The other children trusted Him and followed where He led.

But I refused to listen, and sought another trail,

Ignoring lessons left me lost, and starving, weak and frail,

I tripped and fell on beds of thorns and bled till pain was gone,

Then wallowed in my own regret, exhausted on the lawn.

Broken and alone.

No hand to hold, away from home.

The consequence, my choice.

The silent suffering of a fool,

Who failed to heed His voice.

Once I had turned and gotten burned,

My once was not enough.

And thus began repeated sins,

My tender soul made tough.

The hardened stone, when left alone, found once was not enough.

BEDSIDE

Her eyes were framed with wisdom,

Her body pale and gaunt.

Behind her mound of pillows,

A sanctum free of want.

Those bleached for care attended her,

And quickly did their chores.

The eyes with tears were held at bay;

Is this what God ignores?

She takes a breath through drying lips,

Then grasps a loved one's hand.

The time for talk had passed us by,

As if it all was planned.

We lingered at her bedside,

And prayed for her relief.

She shared a calming radiance,

The fruits of her belief.

I read the psalm she knew by heart;

She nodded once and smiled.

Our sacred vigil ended soon,

Once all was reconciled.

Her vows were kept, so then she slept,

How well she'd played her part.

Swept up by unseen escorts,

We watched her soul depart.

The bed that now is empty

Embraced a life lived well.

Will we step up and follow?

Now only time will tell.

DAWN

The crystal dew on blades of grass

Reflected morning's breath.

And orange sunrays lit the hills

That hours of darkness left.

As tiny sparrows skimmed and plunged

Through shallow layered mist,

Eternal lovers of the slopes

Drew hearts on faces kissed.

The aging logs along the bank

Subdued the ripples growth,

While chimes of dawn and evenings gone exchanged their
reverent oath.

For night had dashed,

When daylight flashed in bursts of blinding warmth,

And we awoke together.

THE CALMING

Like passionate moonlight that quivers the sea,

And mist that subdues every wave,

Your translucent glimmers have brightened my world,

Paling the anger in me.

I've buried blind hatred that closely I knew, though not as a friend, but a foe.

WAITING FOR WARMTH

When was the day there was peace?

When did we see clouds of dust in the sky,

While stretching on grass to watch pollen float by?

It was the spring, as I recall,

That is, if it was any time at all.

It was in the spring that we knew.

We don't tell the cynics these things.

They laugh.

They laugh like those who've never cried,

Or felt the wondrous pain inside...

Of complete contentment.

I cannot claim to know this world,

And yet, we both have seen,

How friendships we've made,

Like frost is displayed

When spreading on cold window glass.

Those dark mornings past,

They could never last, once spring brought the best warmth
of all.

I'VE HEARD IT SAID

I'm told that it was long ago,

When chaos plagued the world,

And warriors armored head to toe

Defended flags unfurled.

All hopes of true repentance died

As pompous leaders swore

That they would smite the enemies

That righteous souls abhor.

The gods of evil triumphed,

Not content in taking lives,

Or disemboweling children,

Or mutilating wives.

They used their cunning mavens

With voices shrill but clear,

Persuasive and convincing,

Seductive to the ear.

The masses bowed

Within the cloud

And pledged aloud

To join the crowd.

But once the dust had settled there,

On gruesome battlefields bare,

The widows stayed to grieve and stare,

And keep their infants fed.

Their world was dead.

Or so I've heard it said.

I'm told that it was long ago,

When echoes filled the skies.

With faint regretful sighs,

And weary tearful eyes refused to see the lies.

I'm told that it was long ago.

But now I know how such things go.

Voices of deception will always find reception.

ADVENTING

Look a little closer.

You'll see my smiling eyes.

My passionate disguise for thoughtfulness.

Most people look and miss the trace

Of shallow laugh lines on my face,

That serve to map my every trait for those who know my years.

And you, who know my fears,

Will grasp my hand and walk the mall,

And count the portraits on the wall

Of neighbors never known at all.

The frame of every window scene will catch the dust.

It must...

To document this season of unbridled, senseless reason.

While beggars in the street

Still linger at our feet,

And crave our sugared treat.

We loners in the mall,

Together we could help them all.

THE RIDE

And I, on my rocking horse, come to a stop,

To study the grain of the wood,

To count all the rings in the trunks of the trees,

Till aging can be understood.

I gaze at the blessings my foundation holds,

Some artifacts cracking from misshapen molds,

While circles form under my eyes.

I pet my old steed,

Settled firm on my mount...

And ride...

And ride...

And ride...

To canyons cut in walls of stone,

With exits that are all unknown,

I ride on slowly, all alone.

Is there any consolation?

THE FARAWAY LAND NEARBY

Come to my window and have a look in, at fairylike people
with cantaloupe skin.

Their land is a small one, with mountains and seas, and
animals tiny that dwell in the trees.

Their king is a ruler, divine and supreme, who feasts on his
money and marshmallow cream.

His courtyards and castles, resplendent though gaunt, boast
multiple banners; his colors they flaunt.

The migrants and peasants sleep soundly on bundles of straw
on the earth.

While knight-slaying dragons fly searching for children fair
maidens gave birth.

For centuries passing, their life stayed the same,

The merchants would sell to the travelers who came.

The mornings were orange, the evenings were pink,

And smithies were judged by their chainage in link.

The barter was passed as the young people wed,

And great celebrations were held for the dead.

The killers were punished by rope round the throat,

And enemies savage were drowned in the moat.

The brothels are closed by decree of the king for their unstifled practice of sin-profiting.

The Navy gives honors for pirates they slay on dark windy seas far away.

And cast-golden medals are chested by every young sailor well-tested.

Now sorrow and grief, as decreed by the king, are heard as flames billow to burn everything.

Oh, famine and death, let them suffer no more.

Lost lives by the millions and souls by the score.

Please bring them the proud ruler's head on a platter with champagne and bread.

Or maybe, instead...bring his crown.

Today it lies barren, the land swept by sin,

The land of the people with cantaloupe skin.

Their temples are ruined, their armies are gone,

Their peppermint candles had melted by dawn.

Yet off in the steeple that's left of a church,

Three figures chant murmurs from pews where they perch.

And in a dark corner, with stained quills in hand,

Are elders recording the fall of their land.

Small seeds that were scattered continue to grow in trenches and foxholes now buried in snow.

And answers to questions we never will know...fade softly...as rises the fog.

THE LEGEND

The wrinkled old crooner stared long at The Bay,

Preparing to broadcast his special today.

The middle-aged mistresses swarm him, I'm told,

And follow his wagon in corsets of gold...

Yet merely to prove they are younger than old.

Gone are his resonant tones.

His platters once sold out like pancakes, I hear,

And targeted drinkers once purchased his beer.

Now darkens and thickens his hair by the year,

And orchestras cover his moans.

Why does he keep running a young sprinter's dash,

When he can retire and count all his cash?

What's keeping him going?

What does he think?

Addressing these questions would drain all my ink.

He's lost in The Newest Thing's world.

No doubt, he will sing on as dying fans cling on.

For all crooners slumbered once encores were numbered.

THE MARM

My ancient school of years gone by stands lifeless on the hill.

Dare I creep inside her walls and rouse her spirits still?

I smell her paint, so drab and faint,

It lingers in the air,

Where nameless men with smiling eyes

Swept dirt from here to there.

Her desks are random warriors who fought relentless heat

from rusty radiator coils perched low on lion's feet.

The shifting light responds on cue to movements in the sky;

And illustrates the cracking walls patched up in days gone by.

Now time tears mortar from her walls to rain debris on stairway crawls,

While echoes that the night installs bounce madly room to room.

Back in a corner, crouched beneath an endless youth of dreamful sleep,

A shadow sways throughout the maze in search of broken hearts.

Yet now the silent matron sits so proudly in the dew,

As moonlight wraps her sagging eaves where mating pigeons coo.

The stoic elms surround her still and reach to touch her face.

They are the living witnesses of what was once her place.

For some, she was a savior, a cherished memory womb.

For some, she was a prison, a loathsome memory tomb.

What was she then? What is she now?

Her fruits will surely tell. The outcome of her lessons will, in us, be tested well.

MORE LORE

Don't line my clouds with silver,

Nor plate my pain with gold,

Nor flatter every dilletante,

Nor cast aside the old.

Just climb a tree to barefoot be,

Way up beyond the earth.

I am a misplaced throwback,

A lone romantic rube,

Who finds his rest in satin arms,

And sifts the air for fleeting charms,

In moonlight solitude.

I know the longings of my heart,

But mindfulness is where I start.

My wistful thoughts are poet's lore,

And you're the one I write them for.

They may be waste to modern man and dross to mammon's rolls,

But rhyming in the voice of verse brings joy to playful souls.

BY AND BY

By and by, I awoke, to find myself parched on a pillow alone,

In search of the maiden I always have known to be lying beside me in sleep.

Surveillance of the countryside 'neath warmer covers safe inside,

Gave reason for my passing doubts that sunrise ever comes.

The wall by the garden casts shadows upon

The clover that captures the dampness of dawn,

And there, by the well, in bright scarlet robe, I see my missing maid.

This is the spring, the beautiful spring,

With sun beaming gold in her hair.

Her head seems to sway, first near then away, in the cool of the Swiss morning air.

She picks flowers for vases we've made,

While concealing the traces we've laid.

Our summer retreat and the times when we meet are secretly left where we've stayed.

Now, no matter how long or how wrong they may search, they will never be able to explain our sudden disappearance.

THE SWIMMER

The virtues of the swimmer were displayed in fine technique,

Once lauded as a hero at his high athletic peak.

His attributes of ageless grace had skimmed the churning water's face and captured victories from disgrace.

What docile demons lurked beneath the wake behind his flailing feet?

Does the dark depth disappear, along with every swimmer's fear, when terrestrials compete?

For there through the murk at the bottom,

A faint silhouette can be seen.

A listless and lone drowning floater,

Once powered by muscular lean.

As holiday crowds scurry down to the sea,

To romp in the sun and the sand,

A paddler discovers a pale lifeless man with clutches of kelp in his hand.

Soon the sunbathers surround him, feeling helpless and shaking with sighs.

They'll never escape what they've witnessed:

The death stare of glaze in those eyes.

THE PATH

Our differences amuse us,

And often they confuse us,

But surely God will use us,

As we let these tensions fuse us with His great and perfect plan.

We know the laws of nature,

We know His only Son,

We know that our Creator will end what He's begun.

From lofty heights with blinding lights,

God gives us eyes to see,

The way that's laid before us on the path that sinners flee.

For we who pursue virtue,

And long to be alive,

In faith and fear of something near, we know that souls survive.

Our every word, our every deed, are stanzas in a hymn.

And heaven's light shines brightest as the worldly light grows dim.

Some may fall beside us, but we will stay in stride,

As every step is lighter as we shed the weight of pride.

My hand is merely one of those,

That scribbles rhyme and papers prose,

'Bout wooded hills and billowed skies,

In hopes that thoughts of God arise

To brighten someone's tired eyes.

And here's one more surprise.

It's one you wouldn't guess...

In failure comes success.

PEACE

In sharing, I find distance from these strange and tempered times.

And, in rest, I find a vision of my future of repose.

For those who never get a glimpse of such tranquility,

There is no joy, no calm relief, no soothing melody.

The love song can only be sung within the Creator's grace.

<u>THE BEADED DOOR</u>

Sometime not so long ago,

You pulled away my mask,

I watched as you moved to and fro,

And set about your task.

You gathered up my pile of shreds,

Creating art from fraying threads.

You wove a string of lavish cord

and small green balls of wood,

Then laced in crystals side by side

As no one ever could...

To clothe my doorway open.

How strange it is to have a door

That none can ever close.

A door that scatters outer light, then lets it in by rows.

Now every time I come into this place I call my own,

I brush against your loving care and know I'm not alone.

You rustle my hair with your hand.

HOME

I've built for you a window etched with rows of colored glass.

It once stained ancient churches.

We've settled in the birches in this cozy cottage stone.

The hillside greens are bedroom scenes for eager lovers young.

This is their art,

They've made their start;

It's now a part of them.

How nature gives us meaning.

How loving is her reach.

How wondrous that she scents her hands to touch her fondest each.

Inspired, I ink my paper,

with tunes the lonely heard,

In place of idle chatter, the power of the word.

I long to learn the language of the loved.

I crave affection and protection showered from above.

I clear my mind of cluttered space

As hues from stained glass warm my face.

These panes provide the color in my sight.

But never in the night.

I look at you and smile.

Your resting head has found its place.

Our hands caress the pillow lace.

We have our bed.

Our children, fed.

And now we have a home.

NINETEEN TO FOUR

19/And so begins our waiting.

23/As patient moments fly.

9/With golden horses gaiting.

20/So indigo the sky.

26/The clouded moons pass by.

5/While Jesus shows us why.

18/We'll feel the sun in June.

12/The code revealed soon.

1/To join the dream we've mounted,

14/This secret can be counted.

4/Heaven in eleven.

THERE COMES A DAY

Malevolent spirits have haunted our land,

Infesting the lowly, deluding the grand.

We've swallowed false wisdom and drowned in our dreams.

Relationships ruined; souls torn at the seams.

How sad that we kill to live and steal to give!

I refuse to bear witness for the witless.

I have chosen another way and made my life with her.

There comes a day that ends the gray and atones for wintery moans.

The heavens will open and lower a stair,

For the lovely lady with gold in her hair.

I'll watch her descending with breezes at play,

Fanned up by the angels that show her the way.

They'll spread out to cover the dry, barren earth,

To strengthen the withered, announcing a birth.

Then ever so gentle and ever so kind,

The golden-haired lady will capture my mind.

She'll whisper these words in a song she will sing:

"I'm bringing you three of my gifts wrapped in love:

The truth…understanding…and patience.

Now open your heart, only once, nothing more,

I'll bathe you and fill you as never before."

Taking a breath as I trust in her vow,

Her presence sustains me, from then until now.

And, somehow, I know that not sooner but later,

I'll gaze in the eyes of my God, the Creator.

SILVER FLURRY

I followed Silver Flurry to the sea.

And standing there beside her,

I was never more immortal,

Never more ambitious,

I was made to follow Silver Flurry to the sea!

I followed Silver Flurry to the hills.

And resting long beside her,

I grew restless and resentful,

I turned ever more self-centered.

Why should I follow Silver Flurry to the hills?

But still I followed Silver Flurry to the clouds.

As darkened billows hid me,

I was never so uneasy,

Never so perplexed.

There's risk with Silver Flurry in the clouds.

So off I ran in anxious hope of making my escape.

But Silver Flurry followed, and she wrapped me in her cape.

She caught me in her breeze,

And drew me back with ease.

Was I meant to follow Silver Flurry all the way?

Oh, bless the One who woke me from my wayward winger's rest,

And gave to me protection in the Silver Flurry's nest.

BE WARY

Beware the pious nomad,

Beware his empty tent,

He lives among the dunes and dust,

His baited traps are set.

In endless circles he will run,

Beneath a searing, lightless sun.

Enmeshed in cultic habits,

He teeters on the brim.

And on his sleeves, in full display, are photographs of him.

Within a world of black and white,

His comfort zone is haze.

Allergic to decision, he hides among the grays.

He raises blushes, captures eyes, amusing passersby.

But in the end, he's not your friend,

His converts all know why.

Beware his sanctimony,

Beware his charming corpse.

He dances to amuse you,

Delusion marks his course.

His bitter wine, appearing fine, is poured into a vase,

With dried-up flowers framed around his smiling, fleshless face.

Beware his sweet deceptions.

Beware his shallow claims.

Within his lair, a monster there, that no man ever tames.

Beware the hungry nomad.

Beware his lustful soul.

He'll fan your sin to draw you in,

And then take full control.

Beware religious nomads.

<u>COMPASSION</u>

Bemoaning your suffering,

I stand by your side,

Yearning to feel your grief.

As pain is alone, so is comfort.

I offer you my strength.

I pray I'll never tire.

For this is your desire: strength.

You turn your placid face my way,

Exhausted, pale, and deathly gray.

You lay there listless, guileless.

Will you receive my glancing stare?

I have a pensive view.

If only you knew my love as I know you.

As illness stains our very flesh

With raw, essential selfishness.

We rapidly retreat.

We cannot even meet.

Self-pity pangs repeat.

Please share with me your pain.

I'll take this wretched bane.

I took an oath.

I said, "I do."

And not for me...for only you.

Into this valley low, we ailing lovers go.

To mute a weakened poet,

Will only make it worse.

Compassion knows the highs and lows,

We suffer life in verse.

YOUR EYES

I contemplate your eyes only in daylight,

For then is when their paler blue comes through.

And only the momentary eclipse of an eyelid can break my captive trance.

TWO

The better half of two is one,

The one with whom the sharing's done.

FOR BETTER OR WORSE

At times I weep at your feet.

At times I comfort your head.

I've stooped to lift your bridal train,

Then blushed at the vows that I've said.

I lack your emotional freedom,

Yet crave your affectionate care.

I'll overcome every barrier,

Then trip on the very first stair.

I cling to your beauty while crushing your soul.

I've flooded your pool of despair.

I've longed for your touches and taken them in,

Then winced in the heat of your stare.

Let's guard against famine,

Let's fight off the frost,

We never are safe once perspective is lost.

Let's stave off the pride that thickens our shell,

We see the horizon, but we can't see it well.

How strange it is that forever is eternal...

But never once-in-a-while!

All the more reason to go the extra mile.

And I will.

<u>MIDNIGHT</u>

Twice the chimes of towers toll,

Into my sleepless night.

As countless sights my visions roll from trembling pangs of fright.

All the while, I echo songs my mind has turned to phrase,

I contemplate your finer faith.

Your light protects my days.

My fear may be the most of it,

These torments of the flesh,

When loss becomes a gnawing threat,

And wounds are ever fresh.

There may be those who sinless be,

But not so me.

Not so me.

All the while, I hear the lines my conscience turns to rhyme.

And that is when I feel your breath,

Defeating death,

Restoring peaceful time.

Why is it that we sleep to dream?

For dreaming is not sleep.

And why the urge to pray for life when living does not keep?

How strange that we suppress the tears that fragile infants weep.

I bow my head as the cold winds blow,

And nod to the rhythm of the falling snow,

Seeking questions for the answers I can never know.

While I dread the midnight stare,

Wisdom grows in the still, dark air.

LADY LINGER

Time your love, Lady Linger.

Sustain your kisses long.

They shorten breaths but quicken heartbeats' song.

Night moves on, Lady Linger.

This midnight magic will not stay.

These mismatched moments, night and day.

The rose in your hand has stolen the dew.

Remember how it came to you.

Those lovely eyes you're gazing through have never looked so blue.

Rest in my arms, Lady Linger.

The rays of light are coming fast.

Our secret passions will not last.

Stay on, Lady Linger.

Stay long.

THE DECISION

There's something in her lasting ways that leads the lad to doubt.

To question every prior loss.

To guess when time runs out.

God knows he wants to mate her,

And formally, at that,

Yet still the looming image of a dark and lasting fear

Brings pain within the ring that now is rolling ever nearer.

Who is this lad to fight the odds?

He clings to infancy.

He'll learn to grow.

And ask to know.

A parasite too long.

Until his strength is gone.

Over-weighted.

Unabated.

Long awaited is the call.

It comes with branching growth, inspired by an oath.

Or is it more the cycles of the tide?

The ocean at their feet is wide; they cannot see the other side.

He stares across the stretch of beach, extends to her his trembling reach,

And offers her his life...to take her as his wife.

Together, they quietly, willingly, dive deep into the churning of the waves.

PIKE ISLAND

The sun peered through darkening clouds as it sank,

Bronzing the lovers who stood on the bank.

Before them the river flowed smooth and serene.

Withholding her torrential roars,

The sky paused from doing her chores.

She held back her rage, setting the stage for the scene.

The moon was surrounded by dim starry light,

To shine summer's blessings this passionate night,

As calm swaying branches embraced them in mystical green.

The river island lovers.

Beneath the realm that hovers.

Just above.

Sacred love.

Close at hand.

In the heart.

Known in part.

Thus, they start.

LUSONG

Across the vast and unkept grass,

A stage was set to host the fest.

Each singer stolen from his nest,

Must now submit to Lusong.

Here we came, an endless chain,

Pummeled by the wind and rain.

Our raspy voices muddled,

We interlopers huddled,

Along the beaten path.

In fear of Lusong's wrath.

Familiar with his lash,

We fight the urge to dash,

Our captive chorus bows and sings along.

We praise our leader Lusong.

We praise his many skills,

We shout his name across the empty hills.

Hypnotically, we join the fest,

As Lusong does what he does best,

He rings our shackle bells.

In strains of broken verse,

We give in to his curse.

Our hollow echoes fill the air.

We sing beneath his damning stare.

In trembling voices raised,

Lord Lusong's name is praised.

But I won't join the chant.

I'm choosing to recant.

In silence, I refuse.

I've seen through Lusong's ruse.

I know the lyrics,

Know the tune,

No longer will I sing.

At once the order came.

"Beat the traitor lame!"

The keepers do their task.

They do as Lusong asked.

I'm left to be a refugee,

A rebel burnt in effigy.

A muted singer shunned.

But still I have my instrument.

Alone for countless days,

I learn to play in other ways,

To harmonize with other strays.

We form a chorus, locking arms,

Forever free from Lusong,

We boldly sing a new song.

The Great Conductor set us free.

So we have joined His symphony.

Once lost and bound,

We now are found.

How glorious the new sound!

DEPARTURE DAY

Hand in hand,

Upon the sand,

The novice lovers stand.

And cheek to cheek,

They dare not speak,

But only sneak a peek.

Then side by side,

They start their ride,

With guardians in stride.

And give themselves into the hands of The Transcendent
Guide.

THE CLIMB

When came the time to climb,

I challenged looming slopes.

Resolved, I moved from hold to hold.

O'er ledged and crevassed walls.

With vain pretended confidence,

I sought the upper world,

But never had I seen the peak.

I felt the burn of freezing winds,

But never saw the peak.

I paused while midway on my climb,

I paused to cry.

My eyes were dry,

I longed for better sins.

Then leaning at the world's edge,

Leaning from my perch,

I dropped a tear which downward flew,

A landing site in search.

But long before it left my eye,

It slowly blurred my sight,

I feared that I had taken on

A reckless, foolish plight.

Light-headed as I teetered near the edge,

I seized the teeth of solid rock

To fight against the fall.

And there I stretched.

And there I stayed.

And there I prayed.

Beyond my prayer was searing pain.

Cruel, death wish pain.

Beyond my lost endurance, there was pain.

Yet still, the cliff I trusted.

And for the peak, I lusted.

I heard the anguish speak.

The firm command was, "Never fall!"

So up the wall,

Up, up the wall,

The misery flattened out.

Before my eyes, the rock was grassed,

To give relief from dangers passed.

At once I stood, resumed my climb,

With panting, shallow breath.

There still were hazards far above,

I sensed the threat of death.

But then the dark clouds parted,

And all my fears departed.

I briefly viewed the summit,

Ever so briefly, I viewed the summit.

And then I knew. I knew the peak was there.

LADY LUCK

Luck, Lady Luck, ran dry

For the likes of the toothless fool,

Whose world was adorned with photo prints of nudes beside
a pool.

His efforts were squandered on idols of bronze.

His money was made by shearing some lawns.

His neighbors all gossiped, in spite of his age,

Venting their rage,

Cursing his name,

Stoking his shame.

He tripped on his cane,

Descending the stairs,

Confusing his foot for a step.

And doing a flip as he hit the last tread,

Caused unhealing wounds on his head.

Luck, Lady Luck, left him dead.

Enough said.

YOU

Behold the shallow pool,

Where men and women bathe.

Taste the floral water from their hair.

And scatter beads of pale blue

Across their naked skin.

Then join me in the moss.

Embraced and fresh, we kiss.

I never dreamed of you in any way but two.

My one and one is you.

SCOURING

Said one little juke to the other,

"Where's the sun that once poured through our window?"

"I don't understand it," the other juke said,

"There were lawns, there were trees, there were hedges,

We had warmth when the solar rays came."

How sad that the jukes lost their window,

And their glass with the clear, sunny view!

It seems it had been covered over

When the paint-decorator came through.

"We must scrape all the paint from the pane

To have sun-shiny viewing again."

"Perhaps wetted sponges," did one little juke say,

"Will wash painted layers away."

The other juke's frown stretched from left to right ear.

"That will fail, brother juke, so I fear.

For hours we'll be scraping and scrubbing,

Pushing and pulling, tugging and rubbing.

We'll be better off steel-wooling.

It's more efficient to use courser grain,

Steel wool takes the paint off the pane."

An agreement was reached, and the work soon began,

And began, and began, and began.

Once begun, it was done.

The jukes fervent efforts were over and done.

Now the bones of the jukes lay in piles on the floor.

And the paint-covered glass is not clear anymore.

And the sponges lay dry by the door.

One juke was infected by slivers of wool.

The metal-mesh rust had taken its toll.

The other juke tired from all that he'd done.

So, he too expired in the sun.

They lacked intuition 'bout basic ignition.

Steel wool bursts ablaze in the sun.

<u>A PALATABLE TALE</u>

Two little jukes decided to play

on a temperature-plunging day.

They dressed in their garb,

With mittens and cap,

And three-layered-pant on their lap.

Out into the snow at fourteen below

They proceeded to romp to and fro.

Now jukes, by their nature, are curious types.

It may even be said they are feckless.

And let it be known, what causes more dread

Is that jukes can truly be reckless.

True to their nature, the jukes rambled on,

And happened upon a form in the lawn.

"A bicycle rack!" did the happy juke shout,

"From under the snow, see it sprout."

Now what can be done with such an object of fun

On a juke-perfect, sub-zero playday?

So as not to waste a brief, frigid taste,

The juke placed his tongue on the bars.

 "My sthars," cried the juke,

"I thear I am sthuck and it hurths."

"Don't move a muscle," the other juke said,

"It may bleed if you pull it away."

"Pleath hurry, pleath hurry," the captive juke cried.

"Be patient. We'll take things in stride."

Since logical thinking can remedy all,

These two pensive jukes were both on the ball.

"If warm and wet tongues will stick to the rungs

Of a bicycle rack cold and dry,

We'll wait for the spring to warm everything,

And the tongue will be freed with a try."

So they sat through the blizzards,

Sat through the storms,

And waited the winter away.

As days and weeks and months passed by,

The worst of the winter gave way.

The sunshine of spring brought warmth to the lawn,

And heated the bicycle rack.

But all that was left were mere shreds of the jukes,

They had withered from sustenance lacked.

Now the bike rack is their tombstone.

The birds decorate it with dung.

And the only remorse that is spoken occasionally flaps from the tongue.

OUR CLAY

The blind shuffled by us in twos,

Expanding our dim narrow views.

Their beacons of light,

Were beams in the night,

That guided us into the field.

Our spirits were tinted,

In hues that were minted,

By flowers that hinted,

It's here we'll be planted by God.

So rest your blonde head on my shoulder.

We entrust our clay to The Molder.

He shapes us to carry the work He's begun,

bringing showers of hope to the young.

The process is agelessness.

It isn't our own.

He waters the seeds He has sown.

PROVERBS OF PLIGHT

We shattered each other tonight.

We squandered our cares and concerns on ourselves.

We lost our sight and compassion in a sea of embattled souls.

It's worse to lose love than it is to lose life.

It stifles our attempts to imitate purity.

Driven by blame, we follow in the footsteps of a staggering man gagging for breath.

Love has no decomposition,

No stubborn and prideful remission.

It knows not the past nor the future.

Love only thrives in this moment.

Anger restrains resignation, protecting our own indignation.

Peace is a meager subsistence in a realm that is ruled by resistance.

In loving you, I've come to hate your flaws.

But I can only despise that which I love.

And hatred is Satan's hand in God's womb, determined to miscarry hope and faith.

Intimacy brings passion, and passion brings fire.

Solitude brings understanding, stemming the heat of our ire.

Resentment is a product of shame.

The rogue of my errors.

The salt in my wounds.

I must repent to cease the burning and heal in the light.

You are the one who disrupts my repose,

But you're not the thorn on the rose.

You're the bud.

Departing the daylight for prison-dark fear,

My ego is strapped to the bier.

I pray that a word from the Spirit King's throne will silence the deafening drone.

These are the seeds that season the bread of better men.

They cast our childish tastes into the brine.

They coat our crust and salt our trust, preserving what we feel.

To love at all, we must forestall what spoils the sacred meal.

THE COUPLE

We all know the couple living under the dome.

They live in a shuttered celebrity home.

They travel extensively here and abroad.

They manage their privacy, temper their laud.

He's earned much acclaim with the magic he speaks,

While she is the beauty admirers seek.

Yet both know that God is divine,

So they won't cross over the line…of perfection.

Those who share their purpose also share their dream.

We all project an image on the screen.

THE CYCLE

I've felt the spark of anger flash from somewhere deep inside.

It rises with a yearn to burn, fed by the winds of pride.

It grows in size before my eyes, instills an urge to kill,

I've met this rage at every age; no doubt, I always will.

What is it for, this inner war?

I'm searching for the source.

It thrives within my well of sin then drowns me in remorse.

If this will be my destiny,

I ask what God expects of me.

Did He give me this woman?

Is she at war with me?

Or are there tools to break the rules of such insanity?

Emotions set in motion a cycle of decline,

Where what was once our mutual dream turns into "yours" and "mine."

But wait.

We still have one another, enjoined then pulled apart.

Each cycle with its bitter end provides our needed start.

I felt you drift away from me.

You watched me drift from you.

We may deny it happened, but, in fact, we know it's true.

And herein is the paradox that we, as lovers, know.

We've turned our backs and walked away, determined in our pace,

But, in the end, we'll spin around to find we're face to face.

BEHOLD

Once upon a time, I've heard it told,

All the bread on earth was bought and sold,

Then people watched the bakery business fold,

In the wake of the…

Old,

Cold,

Bold,

Green mold.

When starving folks were polled,

Off tongues this answer rolled:

"Never let the bakers hold your gold."

DESIRE, THE LIAR

I've asked for love, prayed for love,

Begged for love, and bayed for love.

But never was I taught

Sincerity of thought,

Or mutual giving, tithes of living.

Bodies can be bought.

For love is the choice of the soul,

And pride is the grip of control.

Truth always comes in an open hand.

RITES AND WRONGS

Rites of Seasons,

Sinking suns,

Lost in orange,

Daylight runs.

Rites of Nature,

Shifting clouds,

Benign puffs,

Malignant shrouds.

Rites of Commerce,

Nightless days.

Mammon rules in ceaseless ways.

Urban empires built by peers,

Garish galleries faced with mirrors.

Stressed consumers strut along.

Caught up in the Rites of Wrong.

Rites of Nature.

Rites of Man.

Witnessed by the great I Am.

Does not compassion cover all?

Both realms are tainted by The Fall.

Once we see The End of Days,

Then we'll know what goes, what stays.

Truth is always.

Nothing's new.

Will I be found among the few?

And if I am, what shall I do?

Bowed sunset warms my face,

I'll pray to bathe in Rites of Grace.

DREAMALITY

Dreams contain a reimagined past.

But only very briefly do they last.

If every person lived in dreams, reality would gain.

For finer visions form behind closed eyes.

Our consciousness is cluttered with the scarring of disdain,

The woken world corrupted by our lies.

But you have gifted lasting dreams to the man for whom
you've cared.

They replay memories made and moments shared.

Those dreams cannot be canceled once I've fallen fast asleep,

Each dream projects the secrets that we keep.

I live in dreams with you, convinced our love is true.

And if I ever fall asleep and dreaming is deprived,

I'll know much sadder endings have arrived.

MINE OR THINE?

Those who know not what they want,

Will never want. They need.

And those who starve but hunger not,

Have lost the urge to feed.

There I stand, with tightened lips, so right, so stern, so proud.

My inner spirit torn apart, for fear I'll cry out loud.

My anguished wrongs and sinful steps spill senselessly about;

The fools who put their trust in me have all been left in doubt.

A man who's won at everything must contemplate his loss.

I boasted, "What is yours is mine, and mine is yours at any time."

My words were lost like pebbles tossed into a pool of brine.

"Once she was mine, we stood in line. I booked our time. It all was fine."

Until it wasn't.

I whispered faintly in her ear

Whenever she was leaning near.

I learned to tempt my tender miss

By giving her a timely kiss.

An easy way to mute her lips,

And hope my faults fly by.

Seductive forces do their best

To lure me to another breast,

To sap my strength and tempt my soul,

Usurping all my self-control.

If I should fall, I'm left to lay,

And pray that she'll return someday.

Perhaps our separate paths will cross.

Perhaps they'll cross, I pray.

If love succumbs to mounting fear,

Am I to leave a signal here?

Will a sigh of prideless breath deter a loveless death?

Yet, no, I say, it's best to wait,

To see if she'll reciprocate.

My healing trust for hers.

If I should fall, will I repent, deflecting lies the devil sent?

Such godless feelings I had spent without her at my side.

Yet here I stand, in sinking sand, immersed in stagnant pride.

Love is not simple, is not fine,

Our worst mistakes are wasted,

Like sour wine that's tasted,

Then shelved to age some more.

What for?

Our lack of age has set the stage,

For dismal rage, or worse things yet.

The worst of which is raw regret.

Values that we bury, don't have the strength to carry

The weight of wrongs ignored.

So how can I instill the will to kill what I cannot fulfill?

My boldest efforts turn to dust,

When I cannot rekindle trust,

And clear away the layered rust that's formed from many storms.

The ancient wisdom that I read,

From sages who have all agreed,

That only trouble grows our seed.

Why were we nursed but never told

That every romance suffers mold?

But, in the end, a heart of gold is God's sustaining gift.

The world's so-called "learned men,"

Push their bogus finds on weakened, muddled minds.

I will not take the bait,

Nor bend my knees to fate.

I'm not content to wait.

I've met the man who stands and offers better plans.

We've trespassed on his lands, but still his offer stands.

His open veins have washed my stains.

And this alone is what remains: The offer of rebirth.

For my part, it's the restart.

The only way out can be heard in my shout: "I place my mangled hands in his."

THE DUEL

"My gun is loaded. How 'bout yours?"

"Yes, mine's prepared to fire."

"Then, if you like, let's take a step and raise our muzzles higher."

"This is so exciting. We do so love this game. I'll fire a round and take you down by taking careful aim."

"That's very clever on your part, but you forgot to figure, that I'm the one who's always been the quicker on the trigger."

"You are sly, my dueling friend, but you're about to meet your end."

BANG! BANG!

"I'm hit!"

"You missed!"

"I fear I'm hurt."

"Then hit the dirt."

"I did!"

"Oh, yes, you did."

"I fear I'm dead."

"So aptly said."

A silent pause ensues...

"I hear no breath…this must be death…I'm troubled by this news.

I've shot my one and only.

Which leaves me sad and lonely.

This game was fun, but now it's done.

It feels like such a waste.

In the end, I've lost the only friend who my shared taste."

OLDING AND MOLDING

A tree, as it ages, grows thicker in layers,

More rigid than ever before.

If that is our fate, I choose to live my life as clay.

As hard clay is kneaded, the warmer it grows.

The more it is touched, the softer it rolls.

It slowly submits and complies.

Yet if, like a tree, clay sits in the sun, never free from its base,

It dries and miscolors, with cracks on its face.

The Potter, you see, cannot mold a tree.

But He'll have His own way with the clay.

<u>DEFYING THE DEPTHS</u>

We flounder in waters,

Appearing so calm,

With whirlpools churning below.

Their streams of dissention,

And tides of distrust,

Lie waiting where landlubbers go.

We cry to the Lifeguard.

He comes to our aid,

Regardless of all the mistakes we have made.

We're pulled to the surface,

Our lives in His hand,

He carries us back to dry land.

We rest on the sand dunes,

Free of the tides,

Exhausted but healthy,

Impoverished but wealthy.

The riptide that preyed on our fright,

Had lost in our terminal plight.

We once were so strong, so cocky…so wrong.

Why were we so bold in water so cold?

Hubris may float us,

But dark powers smote us,

When diving in over our heads.

Terrestrial souls should be warned,

Hubristic ventures are scorned

By the powers that live in the sea.

MY BROTHER THE WIND

I take in the scenery around me.

I see white wings beating in the summer sky.

"He's a newborn member; he's the best of the nest."

Set me free, say I, for I know, I can sing with my brother the wind.

And I can fly.

I can sing with my brother the wind.

The dove is my teacher,

My wings of the eagle,

And the hawk, my eyes.

The Son is my compass,

And without guidance, I lose the open skies.

But I know…

I can sing with my brother the wind.

And I can fly.

I can sing with my brother the wind.

If you long to soar with me,

Up where there's much more truth to see,

Just open the door, He's there and He's knocking,

For He holds a gift for you and for me.

For I know…

I can sing with my brother the wind.

And I can fly.

I can sing with my brother the wind.

STANDING ON THE SLANT

I'm looking for the lost and found.

I've lost balance on uneven ground.

The horizon's turning upside down.

Up is down, down is up, and the compass won't stop spinning round.

I'm standing on the slant,

Hoping that I can but knowing that I can't.

The climb is up and the fall is down.

I'm not on level ground. I'm wondering who to trust,

in this world where nothing's fair, nothing's just.

Clear reflections are an urgent must,

when the mirror's covered thick with rust.

Leaning to and leaning fro,

We're all confused which way to go.

Liars planting, no recanting.

Endless ranting, mindless panting.

It's all slanting...wildly slanting.

Set it right, God, set it right.

Come and make it level ground.

SWEET SIXTEEN

When we were young, we knew it all;

Our ways were good and pure.

Our thoughts and deeds were ours alone;

Our plans were bold and sure.

Our lips were loose, our tongues were sharp,

We huffed and puffed with pride.

But were we in the driver's seat or taken for a ride?

Wild ambition.

Competition.

Our eyes were set on gold.

No limitation or moderation.

Caution is for the old.

We make our way where landmines lay for unsuspecting fools.

The plans we made are a charade, for we don't make the rules.

THE GATE (Remembering Jerry Garcia)

The fog moves in and the fog moves out.

The rhythm of the lost hearts' Bay.

Where the hills and chills of The City's life

Wrote songs where the flowers lay.

It's an anxious wait at the Golden Gate,

For the journey only saints will take.

As your ashes float on the memory boat,

To be spread by the living dead.

The season of the Deadhead tour was not endless after all,

As the sage on the stage didn't show for his final curtain call.

When his crew came by and we all got high,

There were mellow dreams galore.

But when the music died, after quite a ride,

Did he make it to the distant shore?

Jerry G, we miss you.

We wonder where you are.

Did you arrive too late at the Pearly Gates?

Or did you find the Morning Star?

BEN

Ben heard there was future in the West,

So he aimed his horses sunward for the best.

The wagons that they pulled, anticipated gold from the frontier test.

Oh Lord, now Ben's a crapshooter, and a trap shooter, and he needs you.

Oh Lord, you gotta tight rein him, gotta restrain him, or he'll shoot you, too.

Ben knew that every journey west was tough,

So he loaded ammunition, twice enough.

A shotgun he would wield to massacre a field of savage reds.

Ben thought that every wagon train was safe,

So he joined and started whiskers on his face.

But then one fateful day, an arrow found its way into Ben's hard heart.

Oh Lord, now Ben's a crapshooter, and a trap shooter, and he needs you.

Oh Lord, you gotta tight rein him, gotta restrain him, or he'll shoot you, too.

BEWILDERED

Bewildered, I'm left standing on the shore.

The prayers for answers that I seek,

Are merely words I barely speak,

My peace is shattered pieces in my mind.

Walking on the water is a mystery to me now,

The ease and thoughtless buoyancy of pride.

Deep down beneath the surface,

The imitators lie where hopeful, faithless walkers sink and die.

Bewildered, I'm left standing on the shore.

Where once I stood and took an oath to overcome the seas,

I hide among the mumbling Pharisees.

For weeks I wait half-hearted,

Each month has raised the count.

When will my faith fulfill the right amount?

The captor's lies can free me not,

Detained from doing what I ought,

Restrained from trusting what he taught…

I stand bewildered on the shore.

THE LITTLE BROWN TEAPOT

We came upon a little shop with walls of bricks and stones.

It smelled of spice and all things nice, exotic Asian tones.

The shelves were packed with foreign gifts,

And sparkling mystic charms,

That caught the eye and teased the touch,

Awaiting buyers' arms.

Up near the rafters of the shop,

Up on a lonely shelf,

There sat a tiny, dusty form,

Left sitting by itself.

Unlike the more seductive ware,

With colors bright and gay,

In isolation, long ignored,

The object hid away.

So up I climbed to rescue it,

A small, brown pot for tea,

I thought, then bought, the smiling pot,

For Susie Lynn and me.

TOURNAMENTING

Let's go off to the tournament to spectate on the match.

To listen to the roaring crowds where fights and ulcers hatch.

To watch the man with savage strength hold other steeds at bay,

Then boast at post-match interviews, "'Twas prowess all the way."

Suppressing pangs of modesty, he pats his heaving chest,

And taunts the mob by asking, "Has my salary been guessed?"

A panting fan screams, "Twenty-Thou..." as laughter fills the room.

Another yells, "A million?" and a dozen voices boom.

"Three million?"

"Four-and-a-half?"

"A ten million no-trade clause?"

Then the hero nods his head and basks in the applause.

From somewhere in the frenzy, a wee, small voice is heard...

Way back in the locker room, behind a pile of towels,

A little boy is standing near where athletes purge their bowels.

"I came to get an autograph. My father said I could.

He said to hand this card to you, to sign it, if you would.

So could you, Sir, or would you, Sir, take this card and pen,

And sign your name so I can show how close to you I've been?"

The pressmen grabbed him by the neck and dragged him to the champ.

They told the boy to hold his tongue; his puzzled eyes grew damp.

Make-up men were summoned to attend the boy a while;

When they were through, they hit the lights and told the lad to smile.

The bulbs all flashed as words were passed,

The sycophants were done.

The agents and reporters smiled, then said they had to run.

But in that smoke-filled locker room,

That chaos had made such,

The little boy with twisted legs was left without his crutch.

SELF-DEFENSE

I put my defenses in place,

And tried every mask on my face.

Acting for no one's sake but my own.

I sought to hide the tremor in my voice,

To reconcile my choice to love the one who knows I'm fully known.

Knowing you was not my fear.

My terror stared back from the mirror.

I'd lived too long anticipating,

Seeming calm, but never waiting.

I feared the painful meeting with myself.

Evasion worked when laying low,

But this war started long ago.

I sat upon my throne.

I ordered this and destined that.

Dismissing this, ordaining that.

But then an echo filled my ears.

A voice from deep within…from birth,

Stealing pleasure, quelling mirth.

It beckoned me to leave my perch,

And plant my feet on real earth.

Debating whom I should adore,

I threw my scepter to the floor,

And found that I was taunted by spirits that had haunted the hallways of my life.

To my dismay, I learned I had no royal blood.

Nor did I wear a crown.

No jewels sparkled in my eyes.

It all had been a vain disguise.

I knew that I had never ruled myself.

Enduring hours of solitude, devoid of any rectitude,

I summoned all my subjects to attend me.

As they walked into my ring,

I watched the most amazing thing.

Encircling me were friends of strife,

Who'd come to help rebuild my life.

My heart and soul.

My mind and bones.

My blood and breath.

My tears and moans.

My little kingdom torn asunder, a voice spoke from within the thunder,

"I've summoned you to walk the path of Truth."

A newfound joy eclipsed my youth.

I now would bow and take a vow to serve instead of rule.

I then dismembered lies I'd tendered, knowing they would be remembered.

In courtship, I had grown, discarding myths I'd sown.

For God had removed the nail from my heart and driven it into His own.

And this was the work of the one who is truly The King.

WHEN THE COAST IS CLEAR

I'm gonna to take my fears to the famous piers.

Gonna hop on a ferry boat.

As I pass by The Rock to the Marin dock,

I will watch all the memories float.

Love Ashbury or Haight Ashbury,

The bloom is off the rose.

What the quakes don't take,

Let the heavens shake,

And we'll wait till the coast is clear.

From the peacock feathers to Hell's Angels' leathers

These are the hills where the boomers played.

The surf at Stinson Beach is beyond my reach,

So I'll see what my brokers made.

Did we stay too long where the tide's too strong?

Were we lost in the comfort zone?

Was the water cold before we got so old?

Or was it all merely ours on loan?

From the morning mist to the sunset kiss,

Here we wait till the coast is clear.

Here we wait till it's late by the Golden Gate,

Here we wait till the coast is clear.

THE REFLECTION

I can't be the man in the mirror.

I can't match the strength of his gaze.

I can't know the man in the mirror.

I can't know his thoughts or his ways.

I lie if I must. I struggle with trust.

I wince at the face in the glass.

But I can't avoid the reflection it casts.

I've stood here for hours, not one time, but more.

Confused and bewildered, I've wondered, "What for?"

Christ is so often a statue or shrine,

That some starving artist has built.

And I, just as needy, bow down to adore,

In hopes of relieving my guilt.

Then armed to the hilt, I turn to the mirror and puff out my chest,

Engaging the tactics I've learned to use best, my eyes appear tranquil, but simmer with rage.

That can't be my face in the mirror; I am meeting a man in a cage.

THE SOLOIST

We know the vile deceptions of the cause,

But stride among the masses in the fog.

If you lose your head,

They'll lead you by the nose.

So know your heart.

Know your soul.

And sing the melody of God.

The breath of reassurance gives you voice.

<u>COUNTERCULTURAL COUNTING</u>

While the fat cat's puffing on his Cuban cigar,

He sits counting all his money in a Cadillac car.

And his wife just relaxes because they've evaded taxes once again.

He sinks sizable sums into his baseball team,

Then negotiates a salary with a college dean.

As their stockbroker said, they are running well ahead of the pack.

They may radiate wealth from their manicured yard,

But eat grub that was grown on daddy's charge-it card.

Hear their stereo play as the mounting protests lay in the air.

With so many getting stoned on moments only loaned,

The dude gets richer as he buys a winning pitcher.

Still, the freaks want to speak 'bout an unjust war.

He keeps joking as they're toking, then he rips them off for more.

While every chick's getting sick from the suds and the duds on the floor.

We all live in a world of revolving doors,

And Christ is tired of knocking as his hand gets sore.

His major competition is the artificial mission of the world.

Can we bury the stocks and stash the hash?

Can we lay down the rocks and cool it with the cash?

What will it take to make sense when the threat is so immense to our souls?

As our bodies grow older,

Let's pull off to the shoulder,

And open our eyes.

For here comes the imminent surprise in the skies.

MY WAR

I've walked near giants seeding soil and fainted from incessant toil.

I've watched the warriors conquer sin, then spread their arms to take me in.

But who can win my war?

I've prayed to the Savior and welcomed the Dove.

I've suffered in sorrow while basking in love.

But who can win my war?

I've felt the loss of gains I take and spurned the verses that I make.

I've read the scholars' lofty minds and sorted through the lesser finds.

But who can win my war?

I've witnessed lights that pierce the dark, while watching arrows miss their mark.

I've seen how masters spin their lies to shackle slaves when truths arise.

But who can win my war?

Battles great and battles small; we each will have to fight them all.

One foe within.

One foe without.

One fueled by faith.

One fueled by doubt.

But who will win my war?

THE NEW DAY

One morning we will wake up,

And wipe the night out of our eyes.

All heartbreak we will take up,

To claim the promise from the skies.

Then we will shout: "Peace, shine upon us in the world."

And we will cry: "Love, free the prisoners of the world."

And we will sing: "Lord, come. Restore your world."

On that Day, you won't forsake us.

You'll redeem us as your own.

All despair will finally break up,

When you arrive to bring us home.

For many years we slept, while waiting for The Day.

We left our hopes uncounted and let them slip away.

But once we see your face, we'll be revived by grace.

Somewhere in time and space, you have prepared our place.

You're coming back to stay.

Oh, that will be The Day.

THE MUCKSIE

While walking through the darkened woods,

I met an awful sight.

I jumped into the nearest tree,

Perched quivering with fright.

On the ground beneath me crawled a creepy, little form.

His fur was gray, his fangs were long, his eyes a burning storm.

I knew he was a Mucksie when I saw those evil eyes.

They flashed in all directions, then rose to scan the skies.

Once the critter saw me through the corner of his stare,

His ears flew back, his nostrils flared, straight up stood all his hair.

I kept my wits about me and summoned all my nerve.

The Mucksie crouched, then arched his back into a prickly curve.

Suddenly he sprang at me, his teeth locked on my boot.

My foot slipped out and sent the creature sprawling off a root.

He grabbed his nose and fled the scene in desperate retreat.

My secret weapon proved to be…I never wash my feet.

SHOPPING

I judge an apple by its snap,

A watermelon with a tap.

A grape I pick when large and firm,

And choose the pear without a worm.

I'm cautious of bananas' hue;

Ripe plums depend on color, too.

But when I choose a friend, I look beneath the skin.

I know the better quality is gauged by what's within.

I seek the soul that's sweet and full, natural and fine.

I also know the finest fruit grows on a healthy vine.

<u>LIFETIME SUMMER</u>

Sunshine Lady, summer's at hand.

Loving Maiden, season the land.

Cause I've got to have the dew in the morning,

And I need the summer moonshine at night,

And I long for the warmth of our midnight mystical flight.

Ocean Beauty, lay on the sand.

Whisper breezes only clouds understand.

Cause I've got to have the mist of the sea air,

With the smooth lapping sounds of the bay,

And to see your blues eyes gazing off at the star-worlds away.

Meadow Maiden, clover the field.

Sweeten the spring air as winter will yield.

Cause I've got to breathe your butterfly weather,

And to wade in your lily pad pond.

And I long to lay the night away,

Hugging you and kissing where the fireflies play.

I hope and pray to while away my lifetime summer with you.

THE ROOM

I walked into the room today.

The patients all were there.

Our eyes were darting left to right without the slightest care.

Our voices tossed out "How are you's" and superficial "Hi's."

But not a one would dare to look into the other's eyes.

Of course, we'd brought our lies.

The very best disguise for hiding what's within.

The strong assessed their rivals.

The lonely were ignored.

The timid sat in silence.

Pretenders laughed or roared.

Nobody fit.

And that's the saddest part of it.

We all would leave just as we'd come,

Mostly deaf and vastly dumb.

In bits.

In pieces.

Filled with scars and creases.

We are the actors pain has made,

Like dried up seashells in the shade.

We dodge the sunshine, fear the night,

But here we gather in our plight,

Obsessed to find the cure.

Because we've seen the tomb, we gather in this room.

THE LANDSCAPE

I've brought my brush and pallet,

There's a landscape to restore.

They do not want this once bright scenery fading any more.

The panorama stretched across an easel on the floor,

Soon will burst in color as it never has before.

For years the aging canvas watched the visitors pass by;

It heard the idle chatter 'bout the textures and the sky.

While visual depictions can neither live nor die,

They strive to capture something rare before the oils dry.

The artists make their vain attempts to rapture what they feel.

But seeing's not believing, and artwork isn't real.

So here I stand, with brush in hand.

All I can do is stare.

Who am I to stain this master's dream?

How do I dare?

I shout and claim the light is wrong and run out of the hall.

But then I hear the master's voice; a whisper, that is all.

He says, "My son, the work is done. My canvas is unfurled.

And I commission you to go paint murals on the world."

I've heard his voice.

I have no choice.

I'm called to use my skills for something more than filling cracks and sketching ancient hills.

I cannot paint the future.

I know I'm not the man.

Instead, I'll serve my patron; he's the one who truly can.

PRONOUNS AND PROVERBS

Youth is a photograph that yellows through the years.

Birth and death will both produce a steady flow of tears.

Time is kept on a pinwheel in ever increasing winds,

And aging is the raging battle that no one ever wins.

Discernment is wisdom's anchor, while judgment rushed leaves rancor.

Marriage is the legal adoption of love;

It gives each hand a glove.

Decision mends division.

Respect fends off derision.

Divorce is the fruit of failure.

Torn seams require a tailor.

Knowledge without wisdom is the degradation of education.

Secrets are arrows, and tempers are guns.

They both do great damage to our loved ones.

The human machine runs on affection;

It's easily damaged when stripped of protection.

God loves us enough to allow the worst to bring out our best.

He never will tempt, but be prepared, He'll put us to the test.

The first thing that I <u>have</u> to do is the last thing that I <u>want</u> to do.

Procrastination is denial when truth bears witness in our trial.

The devil turns our love to lust and substitutes control for trust.

Our intentions won't excuse us if our behaviors have accused us.

When hateful words are spoken, the fragile bond is broken.

THE COST

Reducing life to poetry comes with a heavy cost.

Mere words distort reality like windows slaked with frost.

The vibrant colors fade to dull when buried under prose.

As has been said, no rhetoric does justice to a rose.

Our every breath.

Our fear of death.

The agony of love.

The demons rising from below.

The blessings from above.

The poet strives to capture these, an arrogant attempt.

But doing so will never please nor shield him from contempt.

Distilling time to simple rhyme is daring, at the least,

Like adding tasteless morsels to the Master's sumptuous feast.

Our dreams.

Our schemes.

Our work.

Our play.

The utter pain of loss.

The skills employed to capture these are nothing more than dross.

Put to the test, our lives, at best, are brief but thrilling tales.

And lessons learned along the way are gifts the bard regales.

He stops for now and takes a bow,

Quite weary, worn by age,

He lifts his pen and nods again,

Then smiles and leaves the stage.